SYBIL DECEIVED

CATHERINE BANKS

Sybil Deceived by Catherine Banks

This is a work of fiction. Names, characters, places and incidents either are the product of the author's imagination or are used fictitiously. Any resemblance to actual persons, living or dead, events, or locales is entirely coincidental.

CHAPTER ONE

A TRUMPET BLARED, STARTLING ME FROM MY SLEEP AND CAUSING me to fall out of bed. I stood up, brushing off my bum and wings, and stretched. The sun barely peeked its head over the horizon, which meant that most were still asleep. I slipped on one of my cotton dresses and opened my balcony doors. Others were walking out too, and I waved to them before flapping my wings and jumping off of the balcony. I made a wide circle, spiraling slowly down to the bottom where a crowd was already gathered.

"Sybil!" a female called from behind me.

I turned around to face the green-skinned pixie who was my best friend. "What's going on, Audrey?"

"New arrival," she said with a bright smile.

I turned away from her and pushed my way through the crowd to get to the front where the Queen of the Fairies, Amelia, stood over a flower bud still tightly closed. Queen Amelia was tall, elegant, and beautiful. Her auburn hair shined like living fire in the early morning sunrays and cast an ethereal halo around her. Her white skin gleamed and the crown of ivy made her look like the queen she was.

She turned to me and smiled. "Princess Sybil, come."

I walked to her and sat beside the flower bud, folding my legs beneath me like a lady was supposed to when wearing a dress. "How long?" I asked.

"Just a few moments. I'd like you to open it this time."

I looked up at her in shock. "Me? You want me to open the bud? I've never done that before."

"There is always a first time, and today is the first time for you to open the bud and welcome our new member."

My palms started sweating and my wings flitted nervously behind me. "Okay." I'd watched her do it many times before, but for some reason I felt like I didn't know what to do.

She squatted down beside me and smiled reassuringly. "You are Princess, you can do this. When you see the bud start to shake, slip your fingers between the petals and gently pry them apart. Then, you will see the new child and their eyes will open. You know what to say."

I nodded my head in understanding and wiped my hands on my dress. The crowd was silent in anticipation and I turned, looking for Audrey. She smiled reassuringly at me and gave me two thumbs up. I was about to turn back around when I caught Gerard smiling at me. Gerard was the most handsome fairy in our kingdom and our bravest warrior. His blue skin, and silver hair and eyes were among the most unique of our Troupe and earned him many female admirers. I had never before caught him looking at me and it made me happy. I turned away from him, fighting to hide the blush on my cheeks, and focused again on the bud.

It seemed as though an hour passed before the bud started to shake. I waited until it was steadily shaking and then slipped my fingers in between the petals, and slowly and carefully, pried them apart. The flower opened and a beautiful baby girl lay in the center, covered in a blanket of pollen. Her eyelids fluttered, revealing startling pink eyes and she stared straight into my eyes with no fear. "Welcome, little one. I'm Princess Sybil." I bent down and scooped her up into my arms. She wriggled a moment, but then snuggled up against my chest as I stood and turned to the crowd. "Fairies of the Northern Troupe, I present to you our newest member, Coral."

Queen Amelia took the little girl from me and smiled. "Well done, daughter."

I beamed from her praise and stepped back from her to join the others. Audrey wrapped her arms around me in a hug. "She's so cute."

We waited as the queen walked by each member of the Troupe and then we dispersed to our daily activities. Since I had finished all of my chores yesterday, that meant I had free time. I flew slowly out of the gathering area and to the meadow in the west, and landed in the soft grass, lying down on my stomach and putting my head down on my folded arms.

The sun rose and started warming everything. I was almost asleep when a shadow fell over me. "Hello, Princess."

I sat up and flexed my wings tightly to keep them from flitting nervously as I faced Gerard. "Hello, Gerard."

He sat down in front of me cross-legged and adjusted his sword so he was comfortable. "You did well today."

"Thank you."

He plucked a flower from the ground and twirled it around once before holding it out to me. "A flower for the beautiful Princess as a token of my admiration."

I took the flower and tucked it behind my left ear as protocol demanded. "It's beautiful, but my beauty surely cannot compare to that of a flower, which is much more deserving of your admiration."

"A flower's beauty is commendable, but the beauty of a strong and independent woman is worth the admiration of every fairy that sees her."

"You surely have me confused for my mother or a fairy that is gifted."

He laughed and stood up. I took his offered hand and rose, feeling petite next to his warrior's body. "Your humility is as splendid as your beauty. I must return to the training grounds. May I call upon you for supper later?"

"I would enjoy that," I said with a genuine smile.

He stepped closer to me and picked my left hand up in his. "Then I shall call upon you when the sun begins to set." He kissed the back of my hand softly, bowed, and smiled at me. "Good day, Princess Sybil."

I curtsied. "Good day, Gerard."

He flew up into the sky and zoomed off towards the training grounds above the mountains that backed our valley. I felt like I was in a dream. Gerard had asked me out on a date!

"What did he want?" asked a soft male voice from beside me.

I turned and smiled at the fiddler fairy beside me. "Hello, Charles."

"So, what did he want?" he asked again as he adjusted the knob on a small device he was fiddling with.

"To ask me out tonight."

He stopped turning the knob and looked up at me in shock. "Gerard asked you out?"

"Yeah," I said softly. "Why does that surprise you?"

"I just didn't think you liked that kind of fairy."

"Oh yeah, I hate strong and handsome males."

He frowned. "That's not what I meant."

"What did you mean then? Were you insinuating that a fairy like him wouldn't be interested in me?"

The device in his hands started ticking and he looked down at it and then started turning the knob quickly. "No, that's not what I meant. Stupid trinket."

"I am not stupid!" I yelled angrily as my cheeks flushed from anger. I turned away from him and flew up into the sky.

"Sybil, wait!" he yelled as the ticking of the device became louder. I didn't respond, just flapped my wings harder and flew

4

towards the mountains in the east. I heard a soft explosion and turned to see Charles' hair standing on end and a black streak up his cheek. His devices had a knack for exploding.

I knew I should help him clean up, but he had hurt my feelings, so I flew to the top of the mountains and into the forest. The trees were very old up here and very tall. I walked among them and felt as though their wisdom eased my anger and pain. I sat down and leaned back against the largest tree of all, the one my mother called Grandpa. Ever since I could remember, she had brought me to the tree and told me to speak to it as though it were my lost grandfather. Strangely, it helped me muddle through whatever problem I was having.

Today I didn't feel like talking so I simply sat in its presence. A dark blur sped to my side and then I was being lifted into the air. "Blueberries!" I screamed.

"Sorry, Princess, but we're running a drill here and I was afraid you'd get hurt," Gerard said as he held me in his strong arms.

"You could have just asked me to leave," I said with a smile as I wrapped my arms around his neck to hold on. I could have let go and flown on my own, but it wasn't often that a male tried to hold me in his arms.

"I didn't have time," he said and pointed down.

I looked down and saw a fierce battle between at least fifteen warrior fairies taking place around Grandpa. "Oh."

"I'm sorry to have startled you," he said as he flew over the tops of the trees towards the main training grounds.

"It's alright. I'd rather be startled by you picking me up, then by them fighting around me."

"So, you prefer me to other warrior fairies? That's good to hear."

"I didn't say that," I said with a gasp.

He laughed. "Do not worry yourself, it will be our little secret."

"Gerard, you are taking what I said out of context."

"Or perhaps I am simply unraveling the true reason you are still holding on to me when we've landed safely on the ground," he said with a smirk.

I looked away from his face and blushed in embarrassment as I realized we were standing at the entrance to the training grounds and other warrior fairies were looking at us with smiles. The entrance to the training grounds was a simple wooden arch with the words, *"Train to live. Train to protect. Train to survive."* etched into it.

I climbed out of his arms and straightened my dress and wings. "Thank you for your assistance."

"Would you like a tour? The Queen visits us sometimes, but we have never been graced with your presence before," he asked sooner than I had a chance to turn away.

It was true that I'd never been to the training grounds before and I was very curious about what they held. "I would love a tour," I said with a smile.

He started walking and I hurried to keep up with him. "As you know this arch is the entrance to our training grounds and serves to keep out any other types of fairies, so they don't get harmed in one of our training exercises. Today was a rare exception in that we were training outside the grounds and I apologize for not advising you or the Queen about it."

"Gerard! Why aren't you with the rest of the group?" asked the gruff Commander of the Warriors, Giles.

"The Princess was sitting by Grandpa and I had to save her from danger. I brought her here and she asked for a tour," Gerard said.

Giles looked at me and the anger left, replaced by pure happiness. "It's good to see you, Sybil."

"It's good to see you as well, Uncle. We miss you at the palace."

"My presence is needed here now, but I promise to visit more often."

"That's all I ask for," I said with a curtsy.

"Is Gerard going to show you around?" he asked.

"Yes sir, I am," said Gerard with a smile.

"Good, he's our best warrior and a good candidate for Princess's guard."

I knew I was blushing, but I straightened my spine and turned towards the first building. "What's here?"

"This is the armory," Gerard said as he opened the door and thankfully let me drop the topic.

I stared in shock at the axes, swords, spears, and contraptions that filled the room from bottom to top and left to right in large shelves. "Do we need this much?"

"It is better to be prepared, Princess, then to be caught off guard."

"Is war so close to us?" I asked. Fear crept up my spine and made it seem colder in the room somehow.

"No need to be afraid, you will be protected at all costs," he whispered from closer to me.

"I'm not only fearful for me," I said somewhat indignantly.

"A true ruler never is."

I wanted to ask what he meant, but the group who had been drilling in the woods had returned to put their weapons away. I stepped out of the armory and smiled dutifully at each of the warriors who each gave me a half bow as they past. A few men smiled extra brightly at me and I wondered if they would have flirted with me if Gerard hadn't been there. I'd known since I was a child that many felt shy or as though they couldn't talk to me since I was the only child raised in the palace and the only one born from the royal party mating, instead of from a flower bud.

"Let's head this way, Princess," Gerard said softly. I followed him away from the armory and to the roped off fields where different training took place. From where we were standing I couldn't see anything because we were on top of a hill and only when you started down, could you see what was happening.

"Here are the archery, sword and spear combat, and hand combat training grounds."

"Can I see them?" I asked.

"Of course," he said with a smile. He lifted the rope of the furthest left area for me to walk under and then yelled, "Civilian coming in," before leading me down the hill to a valley where I could finally see the three separated areas and the men practicing in them.

"Every warrior is trained extensively in archery. Hugh is our best archer," Gerard said as he patted the largest fairy I'd ever seen on the back.

"May I see you shoot?" I asked Hugh.

Hugh smiled and pulled an arrow from his quiver. "Of course." He walked away from the target and then lined the arrow up on the bow. I watched his movements intently, trying to memorize them. He pulled the string taut and then released. The sound of the arrow thunking into the target made me turn to look at it. The arrow shuddered in the very center of the bulls-eye.

"Impressive," I said seriously. Hugh beamed from my praise. "Can I try?"

"Princess?" he asked, confused.

"May I shoot one of your bows?" I gestured toward his equipment.

Hugh handed me his bow without further question and pulled an arrow from his quiver for me. "Have you ever shot a bow before?" he asked. I shook my head. "Your hands go here and here. You hold the arrow like this," he explained as he positioned my hands accordingly.

He stepped back and I aimed at the target. I released the arrow and watched in shock and embarrassment as the arrow hit the very bottom of the target, almost touching the ground. "Don't be upset," Hugh said, "Many hit that exact spot their first time and later become very skilled archers after training."

I handed him back his equipment. "Thank you."

He bowed. "Anytime, Princess Sybil."

"Let's go to the next area," Gerard said. I followed him to a large square of sand where five men were. Three of the men simply stood around the edges of the sand while the other two attacked each other with swords. "Civilian!" he yelled to get their attention.

The two men who had been fighting stopped and turned towards me. They held their swords across their chests and then bowed. The others half bowed to me from their standing spots. "Swords are also key in our fighting," Gerard said.

"May I hold one?" I asked.

Gerard looked at me curiously. "Is there a reason you are interested in our weaponry?"

"A ruler must know the weapons she has available for use by her people as well as those which may be used against her people."

"Queen Amelia has never shown such interest," one of the men said.

"I'm not my mother," I said softly. "Though I hope one day to be half the Queen that she is."

Gerard pulled his sword from the sheath on his belt and held it out to me. I took it from him and was surprised at its weight, since he made it look so light and easy to handle. I lifted the blade and twirled it slowly. It was difficult, but after a moment I could twirl it somewhat efficiently.

"Strike my blade," one of the other men said, holding his blade up.

I swung the blade and hit his, but the jarring made me step back and wince. Gerard took his blade back.

"I'm learning that you warriors are much more valuable and talented than many know," I said seriously.

We walked to the final area and I watched as a few men

fought each other in the grass. Their ferocity in training was shocking. "Care to try this?" Gerard asked with a smirk.

"Perhaps another day, when I'm more appropriately dressed," I said with a suspicious nod.

"You continue to surprise me," he said as he led me back to the main buildings.

As we reached the last building I smelled something delicious. "What's that wonderful smell?"

"Have you not eaten Princess?" he asked as he opened the door.

I rubbed my grumbling stomach. "Not yet today."

The building took up a large expanse and held many long tables and benches where warriors ate and talked. They all stood up from their seats and then bowed to me. "Please sit down and eat," I said with my princess smile.

Gerard led me to an open spot at a table and patted the seat. "I'll get you some food."

"What brings you here?" one of the men asked.

There were many responses to that question. Charles insulting me had sent me up to the mountain while Gerard's group practicing near Grandpa had actually caused me to come to the training grounds. Instead I answered, "I've decided I need to understand more about you warriors."

"There you go," Gerard said as he set a plate of food in front of me.

"It looks delicious," I said honestly as I took a bite. "Oh, it's even better than it looks."

The men laughed and went back to eating. Gerard asked, "So what are you doing the rest of the day?"

"Well I was planning to change clothes and then I was hoping one of your warriors would start teaching me."

The room was suddenly quiet.

"Teaching you what exactly?" Gerard asked.

"Well, everything," I said as I spread open my arms to indicate the whole room with a smile.

"You wish to learn to fight?" Hugh asked from the doorway where the others from the fields had just entered with Uncle behind them.

"Yes."

They all turned to Uncle Giles. He watched me a moment as he assessed me. "You wish to learn what they are taught?" he asked. I nodded. Uncle Giles smiled happily. "We are here to assist the princess, and if she believes learning to fight and learning the ways of the warrior will help her, then we shall teach her."

The room was filled with murmurs as the men whispered to each other. I finished eating my food and stood. "That was delicious."

Gerard followed me as I walked out of the building and headed towards the archway. "Are you truly coming back to train?" he asked.

I stopped and turned to face him. "Yes. I'll be back as soon as I change clothes."

"Then I shall stare up at the sky, awaiting the return of your lovely wings soaring back to me."

I didn't know how to respond to that. I'd never had a man flirt with me like this before. I had been flirted with, but not this seriously. I turned away from him and flapped my wings, propelling myself up and over the trees and over the tops of the forest towards the valley where the village was. I soared over the heads of the growers and their fields and over the meadow where I had fought with Charles.

It probably would have been good to go and find him and talk, but I didn't feel like it at the moment. Besides, I wanted to get back and start training with the warriors and Gerard. I landed on my porch and pushed open my door with a wide smile on my face as I pictured the handsome Captain of the Warriors.

"Please, don't run again," Charles said from where he was sat on my bed.

My smile disappeared and I stared at him in shock. His hair was still singed from his device exploding, but he'd washed the rest off his face and clothes. "What are you doing here?" I asked as I headed towards my closet.

"I came to talk to you and to apologize," he said as he stood from the bed and followed me.

I stopped walking and exhaled. "Okay, I'm listening."

"I didn't mean to insult you. You know that you're my best friend, Sybil. I'm sorry."

"Apology accepted. Now please leave, so I can change."

"Change? What are you doing?" he asked curiously as he watched me pull my one pair of pants and t-shirt out of the closet.

"I'm extending my studies for becoming queen. I've decided I need to learn more about the trades. Please, I need to change."

He stepped out onto my balcony and shut my door. "I don't understand. You've been introduced to everyone and seen what we all do."

"I have now, but I still don't know everything. For instance, did you know how heavy a sword is?" I asked through the door as I changed clothes.

"A sword? So, you're spending time with the warriors?"

"Yes, Uncle Giles agreed it was a good idea for me to learn their ways," I said as I opened the door and stepped out onto the balcony.

"So, you're going to learn to fight?" he asked in shock as he stared at me.

"I think it's important for me to understand every trade and especially the warriors, since they are key in a battle. If we're attacked, I want to know what we'll be going up against and what our warriors can do to protect everyone."

"And this has nothing to do with the Captain of the Warriors?" he asked angrily.

"Charles, I haven't even had a date with him yet. Why are you acting like this?" I asked with my anger growing in response to his.

"You've never shown an interest in the fiddlers."

"You have shown me what you're working on and I've assisted you with many of your experiments," I countered. "I have spent many a night with the fiddlers."

"Are you going to assist Gerard with *experiments?*" he asked with such malice I actually stepped away from him.

"I don't know what your problem with Gerard is, but you have no reason to be rude to me when I've done nothing wrong!" I shouted as I flew from my house.

"Sybil, wait!" he yelled.

I flew towards the mountains and ignored Charles even though I could see him flying behind me out of my peripheral vision. I landed at the arch and was surprised to see Gerard waiting for me. "You waited?" I asked in shock.

"I never lie, Princess."

"Sybil, wait," Charles said as he landed behind me.

Gerard put his hand on his sword and stepped between me and Charles. "Who are you?"

I put my hand on Gerard's shoulder. "It's alright, Gerard. Charles is my friend."

Gerard instantly relaxed and held out his hand for Charles to shake. "It's always a pleasure to meet the Princess's friends. I'm Gerard."

Hugh and a few of the other warriors walked out and bowed to me. I waved at them. "No bowing while I'm here to train. Just treat me like another fairy." I didn't really like having people bow to me all of the time anyway.

"I know who you are," Charles said as he shook hands with Gerard.

I'd never noticed the difference between the warrior fairies and the others, but looking from Charles' small frame, similar to mine, and then at the warriors' bulky muscular frame, I realized that there were *many* differences.

"I'll talk to you later, Charles," I said as I turned to head into the training grounds.

"You want to learn archery or hand combat first?" Gerard asked as he headed through the arch.

"Sybil," Charles said adamantly. "Can I talk to you for just a moment? In private?" he said, pointedly looking at the warriors.

I exhaled, knowing this was probably going to end in yelling again. "Sure, but make it quick because I don't want to keep them from training very long." I flew up into the air and didn't stop until the warriors looked like insects below me.

Charles joined me and immediately scowled. "I don't like the idea of you being around all of these males without an escort."

Of all of the things I expected him to say, that was not on my list. "You jest, yes?"

"No, I'm serious. I don't think you should be around so many males without an escort."

"I am perfectly capable of taking care of myself, Charles. I spent weeks at the fiddler shop surrounded by you and your friends and was safe. What's different about here?"

"I don't trust them," he said as he looked down at the men below us.

"Well Uncle Giles does and he's the Commander of the Warriors, so you will just have to deal with it. What has gotten into you?" I asked angrily.

"Me? What's gotten into you? You just get asked out on a date and suddenly you want to live with the guy?"

"This has nothing to do with Gerard!" I yelled. "Why can't you understand that I want to better understand?'

"Because you've never tried to be a real princess before! You just like to lay around lazily and do as little as you can. You're only doing this to impress him!" he screamed.

His words stung and I turned away from him to hide my tears. "Well, at least I know how you truly feel about me."

"That's not what I meant, Sybil. I'm just frustrated and hurtful words seem to fling from my mouth before I can stop them," he said as he reached out towards me

I flew away from him. "I'm sorry you think I'm such a worthless princess. I shall try harder to improve that."

"Wait," he said.

I turned on him and poked his chest, pushing him backwards. "No! I am tired of waiting to hear your continued insults! I bid you farewell, Charles of the Fiddlers."

"Sybil," he whispered.

"That's Princess Sybil to you," I said as I folded my wings in and dropped to the ground. "Farewell."

"Sybil, come on," Charles said as he dropped behind me.

"The Princess asked you to leave, sir, I suggest that you do that," said Hugh as he and a few others blocked Charles' path.

"This is your fault," Charles said as he pointed at Gerard.

"Blame not the one who her attention diverts to, but the one who used the stinging words to drive her away," Gerard said as he turned away and led the way to the training fields.

"Sybil come on, we're friends," Charles said.

Gerard stopped walking and turned towards Charles. "A friend does not spit venom at his comrades. You should learn what a friend is before you try to label yourself as one."

I wanted to defend Charles, but I was too hurt and at the moment Gerard was right. I turned away and climbed over the rope into the hand combat field, ignoring the words that were being said by Charles and the others.

Uncle Giles stood in the grass looking out over the valley towards the larger mountains in the east. "Things are quiet now,

Sybil, but that worries me. The quiet never lasts long and I fear it has been too long already."

"You fear war is brewing?" I asked as I stood beside him, looking out over the majestic mountains and trees so many thousands of years older than even our race.

"I do, but lay your fear to rest for now. I think we are years from it, which is why it is good you are taking an interest in the warriors now. Train hard. It may end up saving your life if something happened to whomever you choose as your guard."

"That is many years away as well," I muttered.

"Yes, well, where are those men?" he asked as he turned around.

"We are here, Commander. We were dealing with a small problem," Hugh said and all of the men laughed.

I should have said something positive about Charles, but I bit my tongue and turned to Uncle Giles as he gave the men orders I didn't understand. "Sybil," he said softly. "I want you to watch the movements they are going to perform and then try to replicate them, alright?" I nodded my head in understanding and faced the group of men preparing to demonstrate for me.

Gerard still wasn't around and I began to worry that he and Charles were fighting, but the men began punching and kicking and I couldn't think about them anymore. I watched the movements carefully and tried my best to memorize them. "You try," Uncle Giles said.

I didn't like that everyone watched me, but being princess had taught me to deal with that. I focused on the grass in front of me and tuned out the men around me. After a quick recall, I began performing the movements. The last one was a jump kick and I tried it, but ended up falling on my butt.

I expected the men to laugh, but one of them simply helped me stand and smiled encouragingly. "We all fall sometimes," he said softly.

I smiled in thanks back at him and then turned to Uncle Giles.

"I think she is proficient enough. Adam, spar with her and teach her the beginner's moves. The rest of you return to your stations," he said and turned to leave.

The male who had helped me stand up smiled at me and held out his hand. "Adam," he said.

I shook his hand. "It's a pleasure to meet you, Adam."

"We'll start off slow, but I won't go easy on you. If you truly want to learn our ways then you need to know how we are taught."

"Agreed," I said with a smile and then stepped back. "I'm ready."

CHAPTER TWO

I sat in the dining area, drenched in sweat, with my head down on my arms on the table, when Gerard sat down next to me. "Rough first day?" he asked softly.

"I can barely lift my wings," I whispered with my head still on my arms, too tired to move to look at him.

"You need to eat and drink water," he said. "Come on, up and to the food line."

"Yes, sir," I whispered as I lifted my aching body from the bench and walked to stand in line. The men started to step aside to let me pass and I shook my head. "No, I told you all that you need to treat me like one of you."

They didn't seem convinced, but Gerard said, "That's an order," and they returned to their spots in line.

I leaned against the wooden wall with my shoulder. "I've never been so tired in my life. How do you do this every day?"

"After a while, you build up stamina and can endure longer and harder days. We all felt like you in the beginning," he assured me.

I picked up my plate and grunted in pain. It hurt simply to hold the plate. I waited in line with the men and received my food. Even though I knew I needed to eat, I wasn't even hungry. I plopped back down in my seat and pushed the food to the side, putting my head back on my arms.

"No, you need to eat, Princess," Gerard said.

"I'll eat after I nap."

"You don't get naps."

I tilted my head and looked up at Gerard. "You're enjoying this, aren't you?"

"Actually, I am, seeing as this is our date."

"Oh no! I'm sorry, Gerard. I forgot with all the training and—"

He pushed my plate towards me. "Eat and all will be forgiven."

I didn't think this truly qualified as a date, but I did as he asked since I had seriously screwed up. Once I'd finished my food and had three glasses of water, I stood and walked to the door. "Would you escort me on a walk, Captain?"

He stood with a smile. "Of course."

I stepped out of the building, ignoring the teasing calls of the men, and looked up at the darkening sky. Mother had always told me that if you made a wish on the first star of the night it would come true. It hadn't worked very well when I was a child, but that didn't stop me from trying even now.

"Wishing on stars isn't something I'd expect a ruler to try," Gerard said as he joined me.

"One must try everything she can to obtain that which will make her happy," I said quoting my mother.

"And what would make you happy?" he asked from very close.

I turned and had to crane my head back to look up at him. "For now, a walk through the woods with you, but my whims change as often as the scents in the air."

"Well then I will try my best to keep up," he said teasingly as he bent his elbow to me.

I slipped my arm through his and we walked through the grounds, out of the arch towards Grandpa. "I never realized how much work you warriors do. No wonder you all get cranky easier than others."

"Cranky?" he asked. "Have I ever been cranky to you, Princess?"

"Call me Sybil," I said as I smiled up at him. "And no, you've never been cranky to me, but then again, today is the first time you've talked to me."

"That's incorrect," he said and stopped walking.

"Incorrect?" I asked. "When have you spoken to me before?"

"It was many years ago, when we were young children."

"And what was said?" I asked curiously as I ran my hands along the rough bark of the tree nearest me.

"A boy had teased you and I told you that I would protect you," he said softly as he followed me through the trees. I closed my eyes as I recalled the memory from so long ago and in what felt like a different era. I stopped and my eyes flew open. "Do you remember what you said?" he asked.

"I do," I whispered in embarrassment. "Gerard, you must know that I was a foolish—"

He put his finger against my lips, stilling my mouth. "You said, 'I do not need your protection. I am my own warrior.'" I couldn't move with his finger against my lips. I felt as though he had complete control of my body. "Do you remember what I said next?" he asked as he pulled his finger away from my mouth.

"You said, 'One day I will be a warrior, the greatest warrior ever, and then it will be my duty to protect you.'" I averted my eyes from his and whispered, "I ran away after you said that."

"And it became my sole purpose for living."

"What?" I blinked hard, tilting my head up to look him in the eyes.

"You didn't see me after that because you made friends with the fiddler and the grower and your mother started teaching you the womanly arts a queen must know. I was always near though. Always watching in case, you needed me."

"I don't understand," I scrunched my brow. "Why? You have many who wish for your attention. Why me?"

"That is a question I cannot answer so early in our relationship."

"Our relationship?" I asked.

"I apologize," he said as he stepped away from me. "I'm moving too quickly for you. Would you care to return to the dining hall to rejoin the other warriors?"

"You would end our date?"

"I would do whatever you asked of me," he whispered as he stepped closer, closing the gap between us.

For some reason when he said those words I felt like I could conquer the world. I felt as though I could do anything. "Would you agree to a rescheduling of our date for a time when I am not dressed as a warrior in training?"

He laughed and stroked my cheek with his finger. "You are beautiful no matter what clothes you wear."

"And you are flirtatious even in the dark where none can see," I teased.

"One needs not see when he has memorized the face of the one he is with."

Wow. I had nothing to say to that. He was so skilled with words, yet he was a warrior!

"Come, Princess..."

"Gerard," I said in my commanding tone. "I told you to call me Sybil."

He bowed. "I apologize. I shall not forget again."

I stood on tip toe and kissed his cheek. "Thank you for keeping up with my whim again," I said seductively.

"If I earn a kiss for each time, then please, make me a list and I will race ahead."

I laughed and slipped my arm through his. "Let's return to the dining hall, if it's alright with you?"

"As long as I'm in your presence everything is all right."

"How did you learn to be so flirtatious?" I asked.

"Aw, that is a secret for another day."

"Perhaps I am not the first you have courted?" I asked, feeling somewhat jealous.

"Your green is showing, your highness."

I hooked my leg around his and pushed on his chest, using one of the techniques Adam had shown me to knock a man down. Unfortunately, he hadn't taught me what to do if the man you're trying to push down latches onto your arms and pulls you down with him. I squealed as we landed on the ground with me on top of him. He laughed and I punched him in the chest. "That was dirty."

He rolled over, pinning me to the ground. "You should not pick fights with people unless you can win them," he whispered. "That is one thing you need to be sure to learn. I do not want to see you hurt."

I slowly moved my arm around and using my wings, propelled us up off the ground and flipped us over so that I was sitting on his stomach again. "Noted, Captain. Anything else?"

He flipped us again with barely any movement or warning and had me pinned with my hands above my head. "Yes, never let a man pin you with your hands above your head."

"Why is that?" I asked breathlessly, from the exertion and excitement at play fighting with him.

"Because he may take advantage of the situation," he whispered as he moved his face closer and closer to mine. I tensed, waiting for him to steal a kiss, but he moved at the last second and kissed my cheek. "I would never take advantage though," he said as he stood up.

I took his offered hand and brushed myself off. "Alright, lesson learned. I can't pick fights with you until I've had more training."

"You think you could win with more training?" he asked, amused.

"The scent in the air has shifted, Captain, but this is a whim you cannot assist me with."

"And who pray tell can assist you?"

I pointed to the men standing outside the dining hall watching us. "Them."

"What can we help you with, Princess?" Hugh asked.

I walked into the dining hall and the men followed, taking seats around me as I sat on top of a table. "You've all known each other a long time, yes?" They all nodded their heads. "Captain, I hereby release you from your station for the next two hours."

Everyone stared at me in disbelief. "I don't understand," he said with pain on his face.

"Now that he can't order any of you around, I want to hear the most embarrassing stories you have about Gerard," I said over the top of his voice.

Gerard stopped talking and pain was replaced by shock and then humor. Hugh laughed. "You heard the Princess! Gerard is free game tonight!"

The men all raised their hands, eager to tell me a story. Gerard opened his mouth to protest and I pointed at him. "Hugh, please restrain the captain. I would be very put out if he ruined my fun."

Hugh patted the back bench. "Sit and enjoy, Captain."

"I doubt I shall enjoy this."

Hugh smiled and said, "Oh, but the Princess and the rest of us will."

"Adam, you're first," I said, pointing to my trainer where he was waving his hand at me.

"The first time I met Gerard, he was practicing with a wooden sword," Adam began. As soon as they heard it, the rest of the men started laughing, recalling the story he was about to tell.

"This is hardly fair," Gerard protested. "I was only seven." The men ignored him and he folded his arms across his chest, his wings drooping behind him.

"He was swinging his wooden sword around, I'm sure fighting some nasty imaginary creature, and not paying attention to anything around him. I snuck up quietly in the grass, listening to him yell and slash and stab and when he was about to turn around I screamed in his ear and made him wet himself." Everyone laughed, including me because it was hard to imagine the strong and fearless captain wetting himself because someone startled him. "He slapped me with the sword, giving me a nasty bruise, and flew off for his house, crying the whole way."

"Aw, the poor child," I said, smiling at Gerard who was slumped against the table with his arms folded.

Hugh laughed. "I remember the first day he came to our Troupe," he said. "He was a feisty boy and decided that in order to show his superiority he would take on the biggest boy around his age."

"And who was that boy?" I asked, guessing the answer.

"Me of course," Hugh said with a smile. "He charged at me, swinging his fists wildly and I sidestepped, extended my foot and tripped the little guy. After landing face first into the ground you'd expect him to give up, right?"

"Not Gerard," I answered with a laugh.

"No, not Gerard. He jumped up and punched me right in the face. I felt bad knocking him out after that, but then we became the best of friends."

One after the other told me stories about Gerard and slowly I was able to picture his childhood since coming here. The more I learned about him, the more I liked him. The hours flew by and Gerard sat silently in the back, smiling and allowing the stories to be told. After a particularly embarrassing story about him trying to impress a girl and falling into a mud hole, he stood up. "My two hours has past. Now, let's tell the princess some stories about you all."

My stomach muscles felt like they were on fire by the time I finally left the dining hall and headed towards the archway. "Were you sufficiently entertained, Princess?" Gerard asked.

I wiped my eyes and nodded my head. "Yes, but I fear I will suffer for it in the morning. My body was already too sore from the training to handle so much laughter."

I started to fly up into the air, but my wings were too sore and I landed back on my feet. "Oh, pufferfish," I muttered.

"Is something the matter?" he asked as he landed back on the ground beside me.

"I can't fly," I whispered.

He walked behind me and ran his hands over my wings. I winced and he said, "You have a rather large bruise. I can either carry you to your home or we can find you housing here for the night."

"Housing here?" I asked. "Where is there housing here?"

He pointed east. "All warriors live up here."

"I'd need to get a message to my mother," I whispered nervously.

"I shall advise her," Uncle Giles said as he walked up to us. "Sorry to eavesdrop, but I was heading this way and heard your predicament. I will explain the situation to your mother so she will not worry for your safety. I'm sure she will be more than delighted to hear that you are working with the warriors and will not have issue with it. Gerard, you may put her in my house as I will be staying the night at the palace."

"Thank you, Uncle," I said with a curtsy. "I appreciate your hospitality."

He kissed my cheek. "You deserve it. You trained hard today and I'm sure you'll train even harder tomorrow." He looked at Gerard. "You're in charge tomorrow, keep Princess Sybil safe, but remember to be sure she is trained thoroughly."

"Yes, Commander." Uncle Giles jumped up into the air and then disappeared into the night. "Come, let's walk," Gerard said with his hand extended.

I took his hand and felt a shiver race up my arm. This was the first time I'd ever held a man's hand before, besides my father's. The thought of my father dampened my mood slightly. I had mourned him for many years and my heart ached whenever it thought of him. A wolf howled and I stepped closer to Gerard.

"Are you scared, Sybil?"

I smiled at his use of my first name and hugged his arm. "I was, but I feel safe with you beside me."

"I would kill any beast that tried to harm you," he said seriously.

"I hope you never have to try," I whispered. I heard loud laughter ahead and then saw the large bonfire with the men surrounding it. We stepped into the clearing and they all grew quiet as their eyes landed upon me. I detached myself from Gerard's arm and smiled. "Hello."

"What brings you out here?" Adam asked.

I turned and lifted my wings as far as they would go. "I've damaged my wing and can't fly to my house. Commander Giles gave me his house for the night."

"Well, come sit beside the fire," Adam invited me with a wide smile.

I sat down beside him and sighed in contentment as the fire warmed me. "I mean no disrespect, Adam, but I am glad I won't be in your hands again tomorrow."

Everyone laughed and Adam said, "You say that now, but tomorrow you'll be in Gerard's hands. Trust me when I say that you will be begging for me back after an hour with him."

Gerard rolled his eyes. "You are a wimp. I bet the princess will be better skilled with the sword than you within a week."

"And I bet she will be able to take you down within a week!" Adam countered.

I looked at Hugh who was sitting across the fire from me. "Is this common?" I asked.

He laughed. "No, we've never had a woman come learn our trade before. I believe you've inspired their competitiveness."

"I believe I've signed my death warrant," I muttered as I pulled my wing forward and rubbed it gently.

"After a week you'll be twice as strong and have twice the endurance. You may be experiencing pain now, but it will be worth it," Hugh's eyes sparkled in the light as he nodded with confidence.

"What is your skill?" one of the warriors whose name I couldn't recall asked.

Everyone has a skill. The growers were skilled with plants. The fiddlers were skilled at building and repairing things. The warriors were skilled at fighting. Normal fairies are sent to spend time with each group to determine where their skill lies. I was not a normal fairy though and thus never went to the groups like a normal fairy would. I did however make sure to spend time with the fiddlers and growers to learn more about them. Now I was finally getting to spend time with the warriors, something I'd wanted to do since I was a child.

"The royal family is not assigned a skill or permitted to discern their skill. We must learn about each group and must learn to do the basics from each, but we are not assigned one like the rest of you are," I said as I continued to rub my wing.

"So, you don't know what your skill is?" Hugh asked with what sounded like disbelief in his voice.

"I have never been assigned a skill, no."

"Is there one you like more than the others?" Adam asked.

I bit my lip. "Royals are not allowed to show favoritism towards any of the groups."

"You have a fiddler friend and a grower friend, right?" Hugh asked.

I nodded my head. "Yes."

"Why not a warrior friend?"

"I was never brought up here. This is the first time I've been exposed to your camp. But I thought that now we were all friends?"

The warriors smiled and I knew it was the right thing to say.

"Let me show you to the commander's house," Gerard said as he stood up. "It's late and we start our days earlier than the rest of the Troupe."

I stood and walked towards him, but then stopped and turned to everyone. "Goodnight." They all stood and bowed to me. I groaned. "None of that! I told you all to treat me like a regular fairy. No more bowing and no more 'Princess.'"

They didn't say anything, so I turned and followed Gerard past the fire and to a group of wooden houses. He stopped next to one of the houses and turned to me. "I'm sorry your wing was damaged."

I shrugged. "It's just a bruise. I should be healed by tomorrow. Besides, it's not like you gave it to me."

"My house is next door," he said with a tilt of his head to indicate the house to the right. "If you need anything I'll be there."

He started to turn and I grabbed his hand. "Would you sit with me a moment? I'm not quite ready for sleep yet."

He smiled and sat down on the porch. "Sure."

I sat beside him and looked up at the stars and the moon. It was strange to think that the vampires, trolls, and werewolves also sat under this same sky. "May I ask you a question and receive your honest answer?"

"Of course, I would never lie to you," he said as he turned to face me fully.

I looked down at my hands and asked, "Do you think I'm a bad princess? That I'm lazy?"

"Your friend was simply upset that your attention was on another male. He did not truly mean the words he said." Gerard's voice was soft and tentative.

"Your evasion of the question is answer enough," I said as I stood up to head inside the house.

Gerard grabbed my hand and turned me around. "Wait, you did not let me finish."

"I fear I do not want to hear your answer."

"You are not a bad princess. Nor are you lazy."

"I do lay around quite a bit," I admitted as I looked down at our joined hands.

"And you also play with the children quite a bit," he said.

"Yes, but—"

"But there are few others who play with them. You make them feel wanted. Do you know how many other princesses played with the children?"

"A couple?" I guessed.

"None," he answered. "Before you, the princesses sat in their palace and had little to do with the regular fairies, but you are different. You play with the children. You are friends with a fiddler and a grower, and you are training with the warriors. No other princess can say that. I think you're an amazing princess who will become an even more amazing queen."

His words made me proud of myself, but it still hurt to think of Charles's words. "I'm scared," I admitted to him.

"Of failing?"

I looked up at him and sucked in a breath. "How'd you know?"

"Because I am scared of the same thing. I am afraid I will fail in my training. I am afraid I will fail my men. I am very afraid I will fail to be the best and you will choose another for your guard." He stopped talking a moment and looked down at our hands. I wasn't sure what he was thinking and I almost asked him, but then he said, "Everyone is afraid sometimes. The difference between fairies is which ones do something about it and which ones cower in fear. You are not a cowering fairy."

"What if I fail the Troupe?" I asked as I met his beautiful eyes.

"I have faith in you."

I smiled. "As I have faith in you." I yawned and put my hand over my mouth. "I'm sorry. It seems the day has taken its toll on me. I must say goodnight now."

He kissed my cheek. "Good night, Sybil." I watched him walk to his house before walking inside my uncle's and promptly falling asleep on his couch.

CHAPTER THREE

"Sybil," Gerard whispered. "You must get up."

"Come back in five minutes," I whispered back as I rolled over, never opening my eyes.

"Wake up!" he yelled.

I screamed, startled by his loud voice and fell off the couch and into his arms. "That was unnecessary," I said as I stood up from his arms and smoothed down my clothes.

He smiled much too cheerfully for the early time. "You have five minutes to get ready and then we're heading to training."

I nodded in understanding and walked to the mirror in the hallway as he headed outside. My mouth dropped open in horror at my bird's nest hair. I would have never allowed a male to see me in this state if I'd been in the palace! I hurried to my uncle's wash room and got ready, using his brush to untangle my hair and then braided it to keep it out of my way for my lessons. I stretched my body and groaned with every move. I wasn't ready for walking much less sword training.

"Sybil," Gerard called. "Are you ready?"

I straightened my spine and glared at myself. "You are a princess. You will do your training and not complain. You are not going to be lazy." My reflection glared back at me and then turned as I headed to the door, pulling it open.

Gerard smiled. "Good morning, Sybil."

"Good morning, Gerard. I apologize for you having to see me in such a state this morning," I said as I started down the porch steps and followed him towards the training arenas.

"No need to apologize for your beauty," he answered.

Was he mocking me? I looked at his face, but he simply smiled at me. We stepped over the rope and walked down to the sand arena. I took a few steps, testing the sand's movement.

"We'll start off with stances. It's important to have a good balanced stance while fighting."

"Adam taught me about this yesterday," I said with a smile. "At least somewhat."

"Good. Now, copy my stances and movements," he said as he spread his legs shoulder width apart and bent his knees slightly. I mimicked his stance and kept my eyes glued to his body as he moved into a new stance. Part of my mind continued to stray towards admiring his body, but I reprimanded myself again and again to stay focused on learning, not admiring his figure.

The stances seemed easy, but then he started adding movement and soon we were fighting imaginary enemies with invisible swords. My body's aching increased until I was sweating from the exertion and pain, not the weather which was blessedly cool.

"Okay, take a water break," he said as he pulled a water bag from a box next to the arena. I took the bag and drank heavily from it. "Not so fast," he chastised as he took the bag back. "You'll give yourself a cramp if you drink too much."

I walked to the grass and collapsed onto my back, looking up at the blue sky and fluffy white clouds overhead. "I should have done more running when I was growing up and less flying."

Gerard sat next to me. "It's a tough life, but after a few weeks you'll be in great shape and able to at least hold your own against us. At least for a minute or two."

"Did you ever regret being skilled in this trade over another? I mean, did you ever wish you had become a grower instead?"

"The only time I was ever jealous of the other trades is when I saw you visiting them and becoming friends with their members," he answered softly.

A male yelled a war cry nearby and then he was over me. I rolled away from his punch, which hit the ground where my head had just been. Gerard grabbed the male's arm and spun him around until he had him in a choke hold. "Too early," Gerard whispered. "It's not time for this yet."

The male nodded his head and Gerard released him. "Nice roll, Sybil," the male said with a smile as he turned and walked away.

I watched him go and then looked at Gerard, eyes wide. "You're letting him go?"

"In our training we have random attacks to keep us on our toes and better prepare us. Usually we do this the second day with our newest trainees, but you aren't as ready as most of our trainees are."

I exhaled in relief. "Oh, okay."

"I would never allow someone who had truly tried to attack you to walk away."

"I do not think I am so worthy of your attention," I said as I turned away from him to look out at the mountains.

"And who would be more worthy of my attention, than the female I have been training for since I came here?"

"You don't even know me," I whispered.

"I know you better than you think, but I agree that I need to get to know you better." He let his words hang in the air a minute and then said, "Okay, back to training."

I rolled my neck on my shoulders and took a ready stance. Gerard made minor adjustments to my stance and then showed me how to slash, strike, parry, and use two hands to attack over-head with an invisible sword. Gerard's skill was truly amazing even without a sword. I knew I'd never be able to become as skilled as him, but I hoped that one day I might be able to at least stand against him for a few minutes in a fight.

After another twenty minutes of imaginary swords, he finally grabbed wooden swords and tossed one to me. "I want you to attack me. I'll only defend, but I want you to use the techniques and stances I've taught you."

I nodded my head and faced off against him. Now was my chance to prove I was a capable learner and that he could push me harder and teach me more. I didn't know how long I could stay with the warriors, but I wanted to learn as much as I could with them while I was here. I moved forward, slashing sideways at him, trying to hit his arm, but his sword was up and blocking mine before I made contact with his flesh. I stepped back and then attacked quickly, hoping to catch him off guard, but the captain was too quick. I attacked again and again, but my sword was always blocked by his. Sweat ran down my face and my breathing was erratic as I continued my attacks.

I switched to a double-handed grip and swung from over-head, but he dropped his sword and caught my hands with his. "Lunch time," he whispered from inches away from my face.

I swallowed and tried my best to keep my desire to kiss his lips hidden. "Okay."

He looked over my face a moment and then released my hands and stepped back. "You're a quick learner. I'm impressed with how much you've learned already."

"I have great teachers," I said as I headed up the hill.

"Sybil. Gerard." Uncle Giles called. "There you are. The queen has asked for your presence for lunch."

"Okay, I have to get washed up first," I answered as I turned to tell Gerard goodbye.

"Gerard you'll need to clean up as well," Uncle Giles said with a suspicious smile.

"Me? She asked for me?" he asked in shock.

Uncle Giles nodded his head. "Yes, now both of you hurry."

"I can't fly yet," I admitted as I rubbed my still sore wing.

"I can fetch clothes and fly you to your house, if you want," Gerard offered.

"No, I'll take her. Go on and get ready," Uncle Giles said as he held out his hands to me. "Don't dawdle."

Gerard flew up into the air and towards his house. I turned to Uncle Giles and folded my arms across my chest. "What did you tell her?"

"I simply explained that you were learning about the warriors and she wanted to have more contact with the captain, soon to be commander. I am getting old, Sybil, eventually I will be replaced."

"You are not old," I chastised him. "And you're hiding something."

He picked me up like he used to when I was a child and smiled sweetly at me. "You could always tell when I was hiding something or lying. Sadly, you could never figure out what it was though." He flew up into the air and then we soared towards my house.

"Is she mad?" I asked.

"No, of course not. She just wants to see you and meet Gerard."

I let him fly in silence since I knew it took extra skill to fly with another person's weight on you. We landed and he set me down on my porch. "What should I wear? Is this formal?"

"Yes, wear a dress as though you were introducing a suitor to her."

I gasped. "How did you know?"

"I've known Gerard since he came to us as a young boy. He never hid the fact that he wanted to be your guard. Or that he fancied you."

I groaned and threw my hands up in the air. "Great! Just great, Uncle! I haven't even had a chance to go on a true date with him and you're already having my mother meet him."

"Do you not find him attractive?"

"Yes, he's attractive," I admitted, not really liking the idea that I was having this talk with him.

"Does he not have a pleasing attitude?"

"Yes, he treats me very well, Uncle. That's not the point."

"I don't believe you have a point, Niece." No smart reply came to mind so I turned and walked into my house. "I'll have Gerard pick you up in ten minutes."

As quickly as I could, I used a piece of cotton and water to scrub at my skin until all the dirt was off and then did the same to my hair. I'd never worked so fast at cleaning myself, but after only four minutes my body was clean and I was able to change into one of my favorite dresses. It took me another two minutes to brush my hair out so that the waves fell around my shoulders appropriately.

"Sybil, are you ready?" Gerard asked from outside.

"One minute," I called as I applied some of the pollen makeup Audrey had made me onto my eyes and cheeks. Pleased with how well I made my appearance in such a short time, I walked to the door and opened it.

If I'd thought Gerard was handsome before, seeing him formally dressed in his military suit made him striking. His gaze roamed over me a moment and then he stared into my eyes with a passion I'd only ever seen males give other females when they were pursuing them. "You look gorgeous," he whispered as he picked up my left hand and kissed the back of it.

I swallowed nervously, but composed myself before he saw and smiled at him. "You look handsome, sir."

"We better hurry," he said as he picked me up. "I don't want to be late meeting with your mother."

I wrapped my arms around his neck and smiled sweetly at him. "Don't worry, she'll love you."

"Her love is not the one I'm looking for," he said then kissed my cheek. No logical words formed in my brain, but luckily, he wasn't looking for a response and took to the sky, soaring towards the palace. The air was cool against my skin as we flew, relaxing me and easing the nerves I felt tingling everywhere. He landed in the courtyard and set me down on my feet. I straightened my dress and set my hand on his forearm as he escorted me inside the doors and to the dining hall.

My mother sat in the head chair with a light blue cotton dress on and looked as majestic as ever. She stood and I curtsied while Gerard bowed to her. "Princess Sybil, I have missed you."

I stepped away from Gerard to walk to her and hug her. "I missed you as well, Mother."

She looked at my drooped wings and frowned. "What happened?"

"It's just a bruise, nothing serious," I said with a smile. "It's all part of learning to be a warrior."

She kissed my cheek. "Do not hurt yourself too badly, Daughter." I stepped away from her so she could walk to Gerard who was still in a bow. "Stand please, Warrior." Gerard straightened and she hugged him. "It has been a very long time since I've seen you. I believe it has been since you first joined our Troupe."

"Yes, Queen Amelia."

She smiled at him and then kissed his cheek. "Let's eat, I'm sure you're both hungry."

I sat down at her left side and Gerard sat next to me. Uncle Giles came in and sat in the chair opposite Gerard. "Where is your guard?" he asked mother.

"He will be with us soon. So, Gerard, my brother here tells me that you are quite a skilled warrior and possibly the best candidate for commander."

"I do not want to be boastful, but my desire is not to become commander, Queen Amelia."

"Oh? And what do you wish to become?" she asked with a knowing wink in my direction. I'd never wished to hide under the table more than in that moment.

"Currently I wish to ask permission to court your daughter," he said with a smile.

She looked at me and I bit my lip nervously. For some reason my reaction seemed to amuse her as she smiled happily. "I give my permission."

Armand, the chef, brought out our food and left quickly. I forced myself to eat slowly despite the aching hunger that gnawed at my belly. It wouldn't do to act uncivilized with Gerard beside me and at my mother's table.

Gerard chatted easily with Mother about current events and seemed unfazed by her presence like others were. It made me like him and admire him even more.

"How's Coral?" I asked after finishing my food.

"She's doing very well and seems to already have a knack for fiddling," mother said with a happy smile.

"That's great," I said sincerely.

"The food was delicious," Gerard said.

"I'm glad you liked it. Be sure to remember to come to the party," Mother said.

"What party?" I asked curiously.

Everyone looked at me curiously. "Are you feeling alright, Sybil?" Uncle Giles asked.

I frowned at him. "Yes, I feel fine. I just don't recall what special event is happening."

"I don't mean to interrupt, but we really need to get back," Gerard said as he stood.

"Of course," Mother said with a smile. "Thank you for coming."

Gerard bowed elegantly. "It was an honor dining with you."

"I hope we see you again, soon, Captain."

"I'm sure I'll see you at the party," he said with a wink.

Her smile widened and she nodded her head. "I look forward to it. Goodbye Sybil, train hard, but don't hurt yourself."

"Thank you, Mother. Uncle Giles," I said as I curtsied to them respectively. Gerard extended his bent elbow and I placed my hand on his arm, letting him lead me out of the dining hall and out to the courtyard. I pulled him to the side of the palace where no one would see us and stood on my tiptoes to kiss his lips.

He kissed me back tentatively, but didn't pursue the kiss. "What was that for?" he asked softly.

"I'm sorry. I just. I thought you wanted to kiss me," I answered as I turned away from him and leaned against the wall.

He turned me around and pressed his body against mine, pressing me against the wall as he kissed me deeply. My head spun and I felt like I was floating. He pulled back and smiled, sinfully handsome. "I did, but I was just taken aback."

"We should head back," I whispered as I stood on tiptoe and kissed his lips again quickly.

He kissed me again and whispered, "Yes, we should."

He wrapped his arms around me and pulled me closer against his body as he wrapped his wings around the both of us. "You're so beautiful, Sybil."

I loved it when he said my name. It was a turn on, on its own.

"Sybil?" Charles called from out in the courtyard. "Where are you?"

The moment was ruined, and I felt as though we'd not get it back. Gerard pulled back from me, releasing me from his wings and I grabbed his hand before he could move away. "Let's just go," I whispered.

"You want to run away?" he asked, his brow lifting.

I smiled and shook my head. "No, I want to sneak away with you to the forest."

His frown stretched into a wide grin. "Very well." He picked me up in his arms and flew up behind the palace and to the training grounds.

"What's the party for?" I asked, my lips close to his ear.

"Do you really not know?"

"No," I frowned. "Tell me, please."

He laughed. "No, I'm going to make you figure it out."

I rolled my eyes. "You sound like my mother."

He landed at the archway and set me down. "Your mother is a very smart female. I'm sure sounding like her is a compliment."

I looked down at my dress and groaned. "Crap, I forgot to change."

"We can train like this. Actually, it's probably better if you train in what you're likely to be wearing."

"Okay, but can we train on the grass instead of the sand so it doesn't get as dirty?" I asked as I looked at my dress.

"Let's go get swords to continue our lessons," he said as he led the way to the sand arena. "I'm going to give you abbreviated lessons because I think you'll be able to keep up and you don't need as extensive training since you're only learning for a short time."

"You're in charge, so whatever you think is best," I said as I stopped next to a large wooden rack which held various types of swords and spears.

"Really? Whatever I think is best?" he asked as he held out a sword to me.

"Within reason," I amended. He laughed and we headed towards the hand combat arena which was empty for some reason. "Where is everyone?" I asked.

"Eating still," he answered.

I turned to face him and held the sword how he'd shown me. "Ready?"

He smiled. "I've been ready for you for thirteen years."

I lowered my sword, shocked still by his passion towards me and then had to immediately bring it back up as he attacked. I blocked his hits and tried to use quick slashes to get him, but he was so much better than me, and faster, that he blocked all of my moves. Put back on the defensive, I blocked as much as I could, but occasionally he made contact, somehow managing only to smack my arm or stomach instead of cutting me. I saw people walk down the hill out of my peripheral vision, but I couldn't take my eyes off of Gerard for a single millisecond or he'd get me.

His sword slid across my arm making a burn and I hissed in pain, backed away holding my arm, and looked down at it as though in serious pain. Gerard lowered his sword and moved towards me and I knew my plan had worked. I waited until he was close enough then swept his legs out from under him and held my sword at his throat.

"Holy crap, she beat him," someone whispered.

"No one beats Gerard."

"You've withheld information from me, Princess," Gerard whispered as he smiled up at me.

"Perhaps," I admitted as I stepped away from him.

"You've had sword fighting lessons before. Yes?"

"Yes."

"By who?"

"By me," Uncle Giles said as he walked to me. "Very nice. Did you use *Damsel in Distress*?"

"A quicker variation, but yes," I said as I smiled at him.

Uncle Giles beamed happily. "That's my girl."

"What else did you teach her?" Gerard asked as he stood up.

Uncle Giles pointed at Adam. "Spar with her."

Adam walked over. "Okay, but I did this with her yesterday."

"Just do it."

Adam stood in front of me and I hiked up my dress, holding one side with one hand and holding my other hand up to my face. "Ready?" he asked.

I nodded my head. "Ready."

Adam lunged forward and I sidestepped him, spinning

around and kicking him in the back as he went by. He stumbled forward, but didn't fall and spun around, ready for my attack. I held back, watching him and waiting for his move. It'd been a long time since Uncle's lessons, so I wasn't completely up to speed on the moves yet. That's why I'd learned the ones Adam had taught me yesterday. He swung at me and I ducked, sending an upper cut into his stomach as I did. He gasped for breath and stepped back. "What the...? How much training does she have?" he asked Uncle Giles as he caught his air again.

Uncle Giles smiled. "That is for Princess Sybil and me to know alone."

"Why did you teach her to fight?" Gerard asked.

"She has always been a fighter, but females are not allowed to join the warriors. So, I taught her in the palace where no one could watch. I only allowed her to come here because I knew she wanted to see what it was like to be trained in the Warrior's Way."

I curtsied to all of the men. "Thank you."

"So, you faked being bad at archery?" Hugh asked.

Uncle Giles laughed loudly. "No, she's awful at archery."

I glared at him. "That's because you refused to teach me outdoors, so I learned very little about archery." I turned to Gerard. "I'm sorry. I should have told you, but I wanted to see what it was like and if you knew I was decent at fighting you wouldn't have shown me. Are you mad?"

He looked me over carefully and then a huge smile split his face. "Why would I be mad? It's incredible that your skill is being a warrior!"

Relief flooded me and I released the corner of my dress which I had still been holding. "Oh, good."

"I'm off on a mission," Uncle Giles said. "Captain, you're in charge until I return."

"Yes, sir," Gerard said.

We all watched Uncle Giles leave and then the males

bombarded me with questions at once. "Hold on, I can't tell what anyone is saying when you're all shouting."

"Let's go up to the dining hall," Gerard suggested.

We headed up the hill and Gerard disappeared into the crowd of males as we went. I turned to Hugh. "Would you still be willing to teach me archery?"

He smiled. "Yes, Princess." I gave him the look. "Sybil." He corrected himself.

We walked into the dining hall and I grabbed a plate, getting more food due to my increased hunger from fighting Gerard. It'd been a long time since I'd fought someone as strong and talented as him, and the last someone had been my Uncle. The males sat down and I realized that Gerard was gone. Part of me was worried that he had lied and he was upset, but I pushed it aside and ate my food.

As soon as I was finished with my last bite, ten of the males called out questions. "One at a time," I said with a laugh.

"How many years has the commander been training you?" Adam asked.

"Since I was five and beat up one of my male friends."

"Was it the fiddler?" Hugh asked and everyone laughed.

I blushed and looked down. "Yeah."

The males laughed again and then the door opened and Gerard walked in carrying a long item wrapped in black cotton. "Warriors, I think you know what this is," he said.

The males all stood up and formed a circle around me. I swallowed nervously, not sure what to expect. "What's going on?"

Gerard stopped in front of me and looked at me with his serious captain's face. "You have proven your worth as a warrior and although you could not be among our ranks due to your gender, we hereby present you with a warrior's sword." He unwrapped the item and held out a gleaming sword exactly like the one they all carried.

I took the sword and held it gingerly in my hands, afraid this was all a dream. "You're serious?" I asked softly.

"We do not joke about such serious matters, Sybil," Gerard answered. "Welcome to the warriors."

The males cheered and then I was hugging every single one of them and trying not to cry in joy. Gerard strapped the sword around my waist and then stepped back. "Hm, that's not right."

I took the belt off and then strapped it over my shoulder. "This is how Uncle had me hold it."

The males looked at me strangely for a long moment and then Hugh smiled. "That's a good look on you."

I laughed and everyone joined me, at least until we heard Charles yelling my name outside. I walked past everyone and out the dining hall to the archway where he was standing. "What do you want, Charles?" I asked.

"Can I talk to you a moment?"

I exhaled and nodded my head. "Sure." I turned to Gerard and Hugh who had followed me out. "I'll be right back."

Gerard wanted to argue, I could see it in his face, but Hugh lightly touched his arm and nodded his head at me. I followed Charles to Grandpa and leaned against him. "What's up?"

"Where have you been? I've been at your house and the palace and you're never there."

"I've been here, training," I answered.

"Is that a sword?" he asked with wide eyes and what sounded a little like fear.

I reached up and touched the hilt of my new sword and a wide smile split my face. "Yes."

"So, you're part of the warriors now?" I nodded my head. "So, you've made your decisions then. You're choosing Gerard over me."

"What are you talking about? I'm not choosing anyone over anyone else."

He spun around and looked at me with the craziest look I'd

ever seen. "Don't trust him. He isn't one of us, Sybil. He was planted here as a child to be a spy."

"You're crazy," I said as I laughed. "He's not a spy."

"I've heard rumors that a war is approaching, keep a close eye on him, Sybil. I wouldn't want you to get hurt. I've missed you," he said as he stepped closer to me and his gaze softened.

"You need to leave," I said angrily. I couldn't believe he had accused Gerard of being a spy.

"Sybil," he whispered. "Don't shut me out."

"You can't just go around saying someone's a spy. The only reason you don't like him is because he loves me and you're afraid I'm going to choose him as my guard."

"He loves you? Sybil you don't even know him! And does he honestly think you could like it out here? He doesn't know the true you."

"Neither do you!" I yelled. "Get out of my sight, Charles, before one of us says something we'll regret later."

He ground his jaw together and flew up into the dark night sky. Where had the time gone? When had it gotten dark? I sat down against Grandpa and cradled my head in my hands. When had boys become so difficult? It was only a week ago that I'd been able to play with Audrey and Charles and act like children. Was this what it was like to become a true princess?

"Are you alright?" Gerard asked as he sat next to me.

I wiped my eyes and nodded my head. "Yes."

"It's not safe for you to be alone," he whispered as he wiped a tear from my cheek.

"What was your old Troupe like?" I asked.

"What?" he asked caught off guard by my question.

"Do you remember your old Troupe? The one you were born into?"

"I remember that they were a bloodthirsty Troupe always wanting war. That's why I was so feisty when I first came here."

"Was your queen nice?" I asked as I leaned closer to him.

45

"She died shortly after I joined the Troupe, so I don't remember her."

"Did you know the king?"

"Yes, I knew him. He was a greedy male and very angry after the queen died. He didn't like me because he said I was the reason the queen was dead."

"How could you be the reason she died? All she did was open your bud," I said in shock. "That's a horrible thing to say to a child."

"He was a horrible male," Gerard answered.

"How did you end up here?" I asked curiously.

He didn't seem like he was going to answer, but after a long pause he started talking in a soft voice. "One night the King was especially mad because he lost a war and decided I was the best option for him to take his anger out. One of the females heard me scream and knocked him over the head and brought me here."

I could see the pain he was hiding and wanted to stop it. I leaned over and kissed his cheek. "Thank you for telling me."

He smiled and stood, helping me up as well. "We should head to our houses. Are you going to stay at your Uncle's?"

"Yes," I answered. "Since I won't be staying up here much longer."

"I'm going to miss having you around," he whispered.

"I'm only a short glide away. You're always welcome to visit me," I said as we walked towards the housing area.

"I'll hold you to that invitation," he said happily and linked hands with me.

We walked in comfortable silence and I knew that Charles was wrong, there was no way that Gerard could be a spy. He stopped at my Uncle's house and kissed the back of my hand softly. "Good night, Sybil."

I stood on tiptoe and kissed his lips quickly. "Good night, Gerard."

I had just turned when I heard movement above me. "Sybil!" Gerard yelled as he dove into me, sending us flying to the side.

I tucked up into a ball inside his arms as we fell onto the porch of my Uncle's house and grunted from the impact. Gerard released me and spun around, drawing his sword and fighting someone in front of him. I stood up quickly and pulled my sword, preparing for whatever had attacked me. Two unfamiliar females were standing in front of Gerard. I started to step forward, but Gerard put his arm out, stopping me.

"You're trespassing. Leave," he said angrily to the females.

The females glared at me, not paying any attention to Gerard. They were both beautiful and had the same silver hair as Gerard. "Fight us," the one on the right said to me.

"Who are you? Why did you attack me?" I asked angrily.

"Stop hiding behind him and fight us!" the one on the left yelled. "Or are you too afraid?"

Her taunt angered me more than it should have and I charged by Gerard and started attacking her. She blocked most of my strikes, but I managed to cut her left arm and her scream of pain made me smile. It wasn't like me. I wasn't normally this much of a fighter, but they were trespassing on my land and had challenged me. I couldn't back down.

She tried to get me with a double handed, over head strike, but she wasn't trained as well as I was. I blocked her strike with my sword and punched her in the stomach with my other hand. She gasped for breath and I disarmed her and then punched her in the face, knocking her out. The other female charged forward and I ducked her swipe and kicked her in the stomach, sending her flying backwards.

Gerard charged forward and I actually feared for my safety from him for a moment. He raced past me though and I heard the sound of swords against swords behind me. Two males had come from behind me and he'd blocked them from attacking me. I chastised myself for even thinking for a second that he might have hurt me. The female I'd kicked stood up and walked back towards me.

"You're not going to win," I told her adamantly. "You should just pick up your friend and leave now."

She attacked me without a word of response. I blocked her strikes and stayed on defense for a moment, letting her tire herself out. After her movements began to slow I switched to offensive and attacked her, parrying her attempted blows and cutting her arms in several places. I spun around her and hit her in the head with the hilt of my sword, knocking her out. She dropped to the ground next to the other female and I exhaled in relief. The lessons with Gerard and Adam had definitely helped in this situation.

I turned around to find Gerard and one of the males in an intense battle. The second male was no where to be seen. I wasn't sure what to do. I could try to help Gerard, but then I might just end up distracting him and causing him more harm than good. Gerard knocked out the male he had been fighting and flew over to me, raising his sword in front of my face and blocking the second male whom I hadn't seen, and saved my life. I stepped back behind Gerard as he engaged the male and felt my heart pumping incredibly fast in fear. If not for Gerard, I would have been killed just now.

Gerard fought with the male a little bit longer and then knocked him out with an upper cut while the male blocked his sword strike. Gerard rushed over to me and stared into my eyes. "Are you alright? Did they hurt you anywhere?"

"You saved me," I whispered and then jumped up, wrapped my arms around his neck, and kissed him.

He kissed me back, but sadly pulled away after a moment. "I need to wake everyone up. Will you please go wake your Uncle?" I nodded my head, feeling foolish for my affection in this situation. He grabbed my chin gently and forced me to meet his eyes. "I'll always be here when you need me. And I'll never let anything happen to you." He kissed my forehead and then ran to the first house.

I ran up the steps of my Uncle's house and yelled his name. He stumbled out of the house wiping sleepy eyes. "What's going on?" He looked at the unconscious fairies and drew his sword. "What happened?"

"Two females attacked me and then two males attacked Gerard. I knocked out the females and he knocked out the males." He started to move towards them and I grabbed his arm. "He saved me, Uncle."

Uncle Giles smiled and patted my hand. "Of course he did."

I sat down on the porch and watched as the males came out and tied the trespassers up and took them away to some unknown place. I decided I needed to learn more about the outside world and would have to go to Mother and have her teach me soon. I didn't like not knowing who these fairies were or where they came from. It scared me.

After the trespassers were taken away, Uncle Giles led me into the house and had me lie down. I didn't think I could sleep, but as soon as I heard Gerard talking to Uncle, I fell into a deep, dreamless sleep.

CHAPTER FOUR

I EXPECTED THE WARRIORS TO BE NERVOUS OR IN A STATE OF CHAOS after the attack the night before, but they acted as if nothing had happened. Hugh stood beside me as I aimed down the arrow which was strung in my bow. "You have to relax and release while keeping your front hand still."

I took a deep breath and released the string. The arrow whizzed away and I smiled happily when I heard it thunk into the target. My smile widened when I saw it a few inches away from the red center of the target.

"Good," Hugh said happily. He gazed at the darkening sky. "Let's head up for the day."

I set the bow and quiver of arrows on the rack and followed him up the hill. "Why do you think those fairies attacked me and Gerard?"

Hugh shrugged. "I don't know. Could have been just that you were the only ones out."

"Have there been attacks before?"

"Yes, but they happen very rarely."

"What's going to happen to them?"

"I don't know. That's up to the commander and the queen."

I stopped and my jaw dropped. "The queen? My mother knows about this?"

"Of course," he said with a frown. "She is the queen." She always seemed so happy. It didn't seem like she could know that fairies were trying to invade and attacking us. We stepped into the dining hall and I instantly sought out Gerard, but he wasn't there. Hugh noticed my sad look and said, "Don't worry he'll be back soon."

"Who?" I asked, and blinked innocently.

He smiled and shook his head. "We can all see how you look at him. Besides, Gerard's been declaring his intent to pursue you since he was eight."

I had hoped my feelings weren't that obvious.

I ate and then went to Uncle's house. I didn't feel like socializing that night with the warriors, so I lay down on the couch and closed my eyes. Why would the females from another troupe attack me? Did they somehow know I was princess? And if so, what would attacking me gain them? Mother was still in charge. My death wouldn't gain them a place on the throne.

I tried to sleep, but it evaded me. After rolling around for an hour, I headed out of the house and walked through the woods. Animals moved around me, but kept their distance.

"You shouldn't be out here," Gerard said from the shadows.

I tried to find him, but it was too dark and the moon was in its shadow phase. "I couldn't sleep," I replied as I continued walking.

"More could come to attack you," he replied somewhere to the left of me. "You should have asked someone to walk with you."

"I would have, but the one I wanted to ask seemed to have disappeared."

"And who is this warrior you would have asked to walk with you?" he asked from the right of me now.

How could he move without making any sound? I was very

aware of the fact that I sounded like a large beast trampling through the woods at the moment. "You know him. He's a very good warrior. Very skilled."

"And he's caught your fancy?" he asked from behind me.

I spun around, but he wasn't there. "Perhaps. Or perhaps he was simply the first to approach me."

"Are you insinuating that if another were to approach you that your interest may be changed?" he asked from in front of me.

I peered into the darkness, but still couldn't see him. "I said no such thing."

"You insinuated."

"I did no such thing." I started walking again and asked, "Where were you today?"

"On important business. How're your archery lessons?"

"Could you please come out where I can see you?" I asked.

He dropped down to the ground from above me, scaring me. "Better?"

I stepped forward and kissed his cheek. "Thank you."

He touched a bruise on my cheek and asked, "How did this happen?"

"Advanced fighting lesson with Adam. I let my guard down."

"I thought you were only going to learn archery?" he asked curiously.

"I decided it would be better if I learned as much as possible. Plus, I'm not that skilled in hand-to-hand combat."

"Be more careful," he said seriously as he gently ran his finger down my cheek. "I don't like seeing you injured."

"Would you walk me back to Uncle's house?" I asked him as I turned in that direction.

He linked fingers with me and smiled. "I would love to."

We walked silently beside each other and I felt my nerves settle. I'd been worried about him all day, even though I wouldn't admit that to him.

The leaves blew in the soft breeze and I inhaled the sweet pine scent. "I love the night," I whispered.

"I do as well," he said after drawing in a deep breath.

I stopped and turned to him. "Thank you."

"For what?" he asked.

"For protecting me yesterday."

"You don't need to thank me. It's my job."

"Still, I wanted to thank you."

"Do I get a prize?" he asked with a devilish grin.

"Sure."

"May I choose?"

That worried me, but I nodded my head. He pulled me against him and wrapped his arm protectively around my waist. "Promise me that you'll not go out alone again?"

"What if you're away on business again?" I asked him breathlessly.

"Then ask Hugh."

"Okay, I promise."

"Thank you. I was worried about you all day," he said seriously.

I smiled and kissed his lips softly. "I was worried about you as well."

"I nearly lost control when I saw that male attack you. I wanted to kill him for trying to harm you," he said as he tucked a strand of hair behind my ear. "If I lost you, I would lose the only thing that has ever mattered to me."

"Gerard," I whispered in shock.

He kissed my lips fiercely and I felt his true passion for me for the first time. I kissed him back, his passion igniting my own.

"Sybil!" Uncle called from the houses.

I pulled back from Gerard and called back, "I'm here."

Gerard kissed my lips quickly and then stepped from the trees, revealing us to my uncle. "She couldn't sleep so we went on a walk."

Uncle nodded his head. "Okay. I just wanted to be sure she wasn't alone."

I walked up to my uncle and then turned to face Gerard, curtsying formally to him like protocol demanded when saying thank you to a suitor in front of family. "Thank you for escorting me on my walk."

Gerard bowed to me. "Thank you for allowing me to accompany you."

"Good night," I said as I turned and walked to Uncle's house. They walked behind me, but talked in hushed tones so I couldn't hear them.

ADAM WALKED TO ME AND ASKED, "ARE YOU EXCITED FOR tonight?"

"What's tonight?" I asked curiously. Mother and Gerard had mentioned it the other night, but they still hadn't told me. We walked into the hall and I sat at a table with Hugh and Adam.

"You don't know what tonight is?" Adam asked unbelievingly.

"No, I don't," I said exasperated. "Why does everyone find that so hard to believe?"

Gerard walked into the hall and it was as if the entire room brightened. He smiled at me and I realized that I was smiling at him already. He walked to me slowly, giving me a long time to admire his physique and gracefulness before he kissed my cheek.

"We find it hard to believe because tonight is your birthday," Adam said with jealousy evident in his voice.

"What!" I yelled and looked back at Adam. "No, it's not. My birthday is…" I stopped counting the days and put a hand over my eyes. "Oh no."

"Happy birthday!" everyone in the room yelled.

How could I have forgotten that it was my birthday, especially when it was the most significant birthday of all for the princess? I wasn't ready. I couldn't do this tonight. It was too soon.

"Sybil," Gerard whispered. "What's wrong?"

My heart was beating faster than a hummingbird's wings as fear threatened to overwhelm me. "I can't. I don't. Excuse me," I said as I ran from the dining hall and out into the night. I ran under the archway and to Grandpa. How could I have forgotten? "Grandpa," I whispered. "I don't know what to do."

The leaves on the tree rustled. I leaned my forehead against the tree and tried to slow my breathing. "I have to choose my guard tonight. It's too soon. It's too early. I can't choose already."

The wind picked up and it felt cool against my warm skin. "I know Gerard wants to be my guard and I know he saved me, but… What if he decides he doesn't like me after all? What if he finds another female he likes better? It's not right that I have to choose a guard so young. I'm only eighteen," I muttered.

"Sybil," Gerard called. "You shouldn't be out alone. Please answer me."

"Here," I called back as I closed my eyes.

He didn't even crackle the dried leaves on the ground as he walked to me. "Are you alright?" he asked and stopped near me.

"I don't know," I whispered.

He pulled me away from the tree and wrapped his arms around me. "Everything will be fine," he whispered.

"You don't know that."

"I know that every time I am with you, I feel like I can conquer the world and that you always bring a smile to my face."

I opened my eyes and looked up into his beautiful silver ones. "I feel the same."

"Stop worrying and let's just enjoy your birthday. Every warrior is coming to celebrate with you and we'll have a great time."

"Gerard, you're a great Captain and an amazing warrior, but

what if you end up wanting something different? I don't want to decide your life for you."

"Is this what you're worried about?" he asked. I nodded. He laughed. "Sybil, how many times do I have to tell you that all I want is to be your guard and be by your side for the rest of your life?"

"But there are so many other females that are interested in you."

"And that is sad for them because I am only interested in one."

"But—"

He put his finger over my lips and smiled down at me. "You are the only female I have looked at for the past thirteen years, Sybil. I know what I want. It's your decision now. I won't hate you or be angry with you if you don't choose me."

I wrapped my arms around his neck and kissed him deeply. I pulled back and looked into his eyes. "There isn't anyone else I would choose," I whispered.

He smiled happily and kissed me as he wrapped his wings around us, cocooning us together.

"Excuse me," Hugh said from beside us.

Gerard and I pulled apart, but he linked hands with me and kept me by his side. "Yes?" Gerard asked.

"It's time to head down to the courtyard for the party," Hugh said with a teasing smile. The rest of the warriors stood behind him, most with the same smile, but Adam was glaring angrily at Gerard. I wondered what had happened to cause Adam to be mad at Gerard, but I knew now wasn't the time to ask.

Gerard nodded his head and tugged on my hand to get my attention. "Can you fly?"

I nodded and flew up into the sky, twirling as I did. Gerard flew up next to me and laughed.

"See, all better."

The other warriors flew up into the air and together we made our way to the courtyard, which was filled with all of the fairies of our Troupe. We landed in the center where my mother was sitting next to her guard, Octavius, and Uncle Giles. The courtyard had been transformed into my party place. Tables filled most of the area and a large bonfire took up one corner. I curtsied to my mother and the warriors bowed as well.

She stood up and hugged me. "Happy Birthday, Daughter."

"Thank you," I said as she pulled back.

She looked at the sword hilt and turned to Uncle Giles. "What's this?"

He smiled. "This is something that should have happened long ago. Gerard, come forward please."

Gerard walked up to Uncle Giles. "Yes Sir?"

"Did you present the sword to Princess Sybil?"

"Yes, Sir."

Uncle Giles turned to me. "May I see your sword please?" I took the sword from its sheath and handed it, hilt first, to him. "Please kneel." I wasn't sure what was going on, but I did as he asked and kneeled, tucking my dress around my knees as I did. "I officially recognize you, Sybil, as a warrior," he said as he tapped my shoulders with my sword. "Rise as a warrior."

I stood up and the warriors and a few others cheered, but I could see that many in the crowd were shocked and some of the older ones were upset. I took my sword back from him and slid it into my sheath.

"Let us eat and celebrate Sybil's birthday," Mother said as she took a seat at one of the tables.

"Sybil!" Audrey yelled behind me.

I spun around and barely caught my balance as my friend slammed into me and hugged me. "Audrey!" I said happily. "I've missed you so much."

She pulled back and kissed my cheek. "I've missed you too." She touched the hilt of my sword with her fingertip. "I always wondered when you'd finally get this."

"Hey, Sybil," Charles said from behind her.

Audrey stepped to my side and I smiled at him. "Hello, Charles."

"Happy Birthday," he said as he handed me a box.

"You didn't have to get me a gift," I said, lifting an eyebrow.

"We always get each other gifts for birthdays," he said as he smiled shyly.

I hugged him and kissed his cheek. "Thank you."

"Sybil," Gerard said softly from behind me. "You should eat."

I grabbed Audrey's hand and pulled her with me to the table where Gerard and the other warriors were sitting. Hugh and Gerard scooted over to make room for the two of us and Audrey smiled shyly at Hugh. "Hi, Hugh."

He smiled brightly back at her. "Hello, Audrey. You look lovely tonight."

"Thank you," she said as we sat down.

I set Charles' gift on the table next to my plate and Gerard looked at it suspiciously. "A present?"

I nodded my head. "Yes."

"Charles?" he asked.

"Yes."

"Are you going to open it?"

"Not until after the party tonight. It's a tradition."

He eyed the box a moment longer and then started piling food on my plate. "You need to remember to eat as much as you can to keep your strength up."

"So, what have you been doing at the training grounds?" Audrey asked as she nibbled on some vegetables.

"She's been learning to kick our butts," Adam said with a smile.

"Really?" Audrey asked. "I thought she was just able to beat Charles and me up. I never would have guessed she could beat one of you."

"She had Gerard on the ground with a sword to his throat," Adam said as everyone laughed.

"That wasn't nearly as funny as her getting you with an uppercut to the stomach," Hugh said and the table roared with laughter.

Adam blushed and pushed off from the table and walked away. I set down my cup and stood.

"Where are you going?" Gerard asked softly.

"I'm going to talk to him," I said as I walked away. "I'll be right back." I walked in the direction Adam had gone and found him on the other side of the palace in the rose garden. "Adam," I said softly. "I'm sorry."

He shrugged. "It's not your fault."

"Please come back."

He turned around and smiled. "No, it's alright. I'm just tired and worn out from dealing with the trespassers. You go enjoy your birthday."

"Are you sure?" I asked.

He nodded his head. "Yeah, I'm just going to go to bed." He walked to me and kissed my cheek. "Happy Birthday, Sybil."

"Thank you," I said, blinking hard at him.

He looked at me a moment and then stepped forward and kissed me hard on the lips. I froze in shock and he stepped back. "Gerard isn't the only male who has had their eye on you. If I had been there last night, I would have killed those males for trying to hurt you." He stroked my cheek with his finger and whispered, "If it were up to me I'd fight any other male for the chance to be your guard."

"Wh...why didn't you say anything before?" I stammered. "You never showed interest to me."

"The only chance I had was when I was training you, but you said you wanted to be treated like a warrior. I don't flirt with the other warriors. And you were always with Gerard besides that."

"I don't know what to say, Adam," I told him honestly. "This is quite a shock."

"Can't you postpone the decision?" he asked as he ran his hand down my arm.

"I'm supposed to choose tonight. It's tradition."

"You just broke tradition by becoming the first female warrior. Why not break one more?"

"Sybil, are you alright?" Gerard called from the front of the palace.

"Yes, I'll be right there," I called back. "Adam, I just. I'm so shocked right now and confused. I don't know."

He picked my hand up. "Don't worry yourself, Sybil. It's alright. I should have made my move sooner. I'm sorry." He kissed my cheek and flew up into the sky, heading towards the training grounds.

I watched him disappear and then started slowly back towards the front of the palace. Was Adam right? Should I wait to make my choice? I didn't want anyone but Gerard, but was that fair to the others?

"Hello," I said to Gerard as I rounded the corner.

"Everything alright?" he asked as he held out his hand to me.

I linked hands with him and kissed his cheek. "Yes. We should get back to the party though." I pulled my hand out of his and we walked side by side back to the party.

"I have a present for you, after the party," he whispered.

"You didn't have to get me anything," I said, but couldn't hide my smile.

"I wanted to," he whispered back. "You're special to me."

"Sybil," Mother called. "Come have a drink with me."

I walked up to her slowly and took the offered cup. It was the first time I was allowed to drink the fermented liquid. I clinked cups with my mother and together we drank them in one swig. The crowd cheered and my mother smiled proudly at me. We sat together and shared a loaf of bread as we drank more.

After an hour or so had passed, she stood from her seat and the crowd hushed. "As you all know, tonight is Sybil's eighteenth birthday. As princess, this is the night that she chooses her guard - the male who will protect her with his life for the rest of their lives."

"No, tonight is the night the true ruler is decided," said a deep and angry voice.

Fairies screamed in terror as enemy fairies dropped from the skies and attacked. I pulled my sword from its sheath and stabbed a female who came after me. The warriors jumped into the fray, protecting the other fairies of our Troupe and attacking the enemy. I ducked a blade from one female only to have another kick me in the back. A circle had formed around me of five enemy females and I felt true fear for the first time in a long time.

Gerard grabbed two of the females and tossed them away from me while I engaged the other three. The sounds of swords clashing and fairies screaming were almost deafening. One of my attackers sliced my arm and made me cry out in pain. I doubled my offense and killed two of them quickly while the last was proving to be quite a struggle. She was extremely skilled in swords and no matter how hard I tried I couldn't cut her.

Gerard's disappearance worried me most of all. I knew he wouldn't have left me alone if he had control, but he wasn't anywhere I could see him. Finally, the female faltered and I ran her through the stomach. I spun around just in time to block a blade aimed at my chest from a male.

Gerard dropped down from the sky to land behind the male and stabbed him through the back. "Are you alright?" he asked in panting breaths.

"Yes, just a few cuts," I answered.

A female screamed and my heart broke at the sound. I turned around and stared at Octavius' lifeless body and my mother's beside his. A large male with a jagged scar over his eye pulled his sword from my mother's chest and smiled happily. I screamed my pain and felt tears sliding down my face.

Part of me felt like throwing up while the other more dominant part ached to stab my sword through his gut. I rushed forward, cutting down any enemy in my path until I stood in front of the man. He smiled at me. "Hello, Princess."

I screamed my rage and attacked him. My movements were crazed and my attacks random, but I didn't care. The only thing I cared about was killing him. I used everything I knew about hand combat and swords as I attacked him, but to no avail.

"You can't beat me," he said smugly.

"No, but I can," Gerard said as he attacked the male from his side. I tried to fight too, but Gerard pushed me back and continued his assault on the male. "Stay back, Sybil," he barked.

"You may be older, but you're still not good enough to fight me, Son," the male said with a sneer.

I dropped to my knees and cradled my mother's head on my lap. "Sybil," Octavius whispered. I jumped in shock and turned to the guard. "I need you to help me," he whispered.

I gently laid my mother's head down and turned to him. "What can I do?" I asked as I looked at the blood gushing out of his chest and stomach.

"Show mercy and end my life, please."

I scooted backwards in horror. "I can't."

"Please," he begged. He looked at my mother's body and tears leaked down his eyes. "I have failed my duty. She died to protect me, but nothing can be done. There is no life left to live without her. Please, Sybil."

I shook my head and cried. "I can't."

"If you love me, please do it."

I sobbed and stood up, grabbing my sword and standing over him.

"I'm sorry I failed her. I'm sorry that I failed you. It's your turn to lead. Make us proud," he whispered and then closed his eyes.

I placed my sword over his heart and drove it in as quickly and as hard as I could. He gasped once and then stopped breathing. I screamed and jerked the sword from his body and fell backwards on the ground. I couldn't stop shaking and felt like I was going to break apart.

"Sybil!" Adam yelled behind me.

I turned around and watched with passive fear as a male enemy charged at me. I didn't have enough time to defend and wasn't sure I would have even tried if I had. Adam rushed forward and kicked the male in the side, and sent him flying sideways.

Gerard yelled in pain and I looked up to find him cradling his left arm against his body. The male who killed my mother smiled and then rushed forward. Gerard ducked and stabbed the man through the chest with his sword. "It ends now," he said through gritted teeth. It was then that I noticed the resemblance between the two.

The male gasped in pain with wide eyes and fell to the ground besides Gerard's feet. Gerard hurried over to me and dropped his sword beside mine. "Are you alright?"

I backed away from him and looked around at everything. The last of the enemy fairies were flying away and Hugh and a few other archers shot at them, taking them down as they tried to flee. Fifty or so bodies lay upon the ground, most enemies, but some from our Troupe. I had never seen war before and now that I had, I never wanted to see it again. I never wanted to hear of it again.

"Sybil," Gerard whispered. "It's me."

"And who are you?" I yelled. "You look just like that male!"

He jerked back in surprise and I saw guilt on his face. "I know I haven't told you everything, but I had hoped you would learn more later."

"Who are you?" I screamed.

He looked down at his sword and said, "I'm Prince Geoffrey of the Eastern Troupe."

"No," I whispered in horror and backed away from him and into a table.

"I'm sorry I didn't tell you, Sybil, but that doesn't change anything."

"Traitor!" Charles yelled as he tossed something at Gerard/Geoffrey. The contraption opened and vines popped out and latched onto his arms, pulling him down to his knees.

"Please, Sybil. You have to believe me."

Giles dropped down next to my mother and stroked her hair. "What happened?"

"Ask him," I said angrily as I flew up into the air. "I want him taken into custody," I commanded Uncle Giles. "Interrogate him extensively. I want to know who contacted the Eastern Troupe and who our traitor is."

"Sybil," Gerard/Geoffrey whispered. "I love you."

"I will do as ordered," Giles answered.

Hugh picked my mother's body up and caught my eye. "I will take her to the burial grounds."

"I want her and Octavius to be buried next to each other," I told him.

He nodded. "I will see to it."

"Sybil," Gerard/Geoffrey whispered.

I turned my back on him and walked to the nearest injured fairies and tried my best to help them. Someone hugged me from behind and I turned to find Audrey. "Are you alright?" I asked in concern.

"Yes, Hugh protected me," she said. She turned and looked at Gerard/Geoffrey being taken away by Giles. "Do you really think he had anything to do with this?"

"I don't know. I hope not," I answered honestly.

"I told you he was a traitor," Charles said triumphantly.

I wanted to be mad at him. I wanted to hit him, but he was right. "Audrey, you and Charles need to tend to the wounded. Find the healing fairies and get them here as quickly as possible."

Audrey nodded and flew off. I turned back to my sword, being careful not to look at Octavius' body as I did. The present

Charles had given me sat a few feet away on the ground, somehow safe. I picked it up and pressed it against my chest as I flew into the palace and to my mother's library. I used to hide in the library when I was scared or upset and read the books about happy families and happy beings called humans. I knew there were other books that told of the horrible things the humans had eventually done and how they had caused their own extinction, but I always avoided them.

I sat down on the floor and leaned against one of the bookcases. How could this have happened? What was I going to do? I pulled my knees up to my chest and rested my head on top of them as I let out the pain I felt and cried.

My mother was dead. Octavius was dead. And Gerard wasn't even Gerard, he was Prince Geoffrey and possibly a traitor. My world crumbled around me and I didn't know what do to.

My tears eventually stopped and I lifted my head. I looked at Charles' box and decided to open it, hoping that it would at least lift my spirits a little. I opened the small box and found a metal ball inside with a note. The outside of the note said, "Read after you place the ball in your right hand."

"Okay," I replied to the note. I picked up the ball and something started ticking. I was worried for a moment, but I trusted Charles. I opened the note.

"You never took me seriously. You never took my love for you seriously. Seeing you with Gerard made me realize that I couldn't live watching you with him. So, if I can't have you, no one can."

I dropped the note in shock and tried to drop the ball, but the ticking stopped at that moment and the ball unraveled much like the contraption he'd used on Gerard/Geoffrey. Vines wrapped up my arm and no matter how hard I pulled, they only continued to climb up over my chest, down my other arm and ensnare the rest of my body. I screamed as a vine wrapped around my throat, but my scream was cut off as it tightened, constricting my airway.

I fell to the ground on my side and tried to move, but my body became tingly. A spectral image of Charles appeared from one of the vines to stand in front of me. "What you're feeling is the poison I've encased in the vines. The more you struggle the faster the poison escapes. It's on a time release and will continue to keep you frozen and slowly dying for the next week. The exact amount of time it's been since you ripped my heart out and joined that warrior. I'm sure you'll be glad to know that he'll get off free since he isn't a traitor and never was. I will be leaving, to join the Eastern Troupe and become their newest leader. Next time you should remember not to shun a male simply because he doesn't have muscles."

Fresh tears leaked from my eyes as this new treachery was unfolded and the truth about Gerard/Geoffrey revealed. I would die and he would think that I hated him because I thought he was the traitor. I wanted to scream. I wanted to struggle, but I didn't want to die faster. My skin started twitching as it soaked in more poison. I wished I hadn't yelled at Gerard/Geoffrey. I wished I had listened to him. Now I would die at the hands of a male I thought was my friend. One of my wings flexed involuntarily and the vine tightened, snapping my wing. I screamed from the pain and the vine tightened around my throat until I blacked out.

CHAPTER FIVE

WATER. ALL I WANTED WAS WATER. I'D BEEN LYING ON THE FLOOR of the library for three days and through the pain all my body wanted was water. I woke a few times, since the vine around my throat had loosened slightly, but there was nothing I could do.

"Sybil," someone called.

I wished I could call back, but I couldn't.

"Sybil," the voice called louder. The voice sounded familiar, but I couldn't place it.

"Sybil!"

I knew the voice. It was Gerard/Geoffrey. I licked my lips and debated what to do. If I called out to him the vine would tighten and either kill me or choke me until I was unconscious. If I didn't call out to him I would lie here for four more days, dying slowly. Not much of a choice.

"Gerard!" I screamed as loudly as I could.

The vine tightened and I gasped for air, but none came. The door to the library opened and Gerard/Geoffrey scanned around the room looking for me. His eyes finally found me. "Sybil!" he yelled.

I tried to stay conscious. I tried to look at him, but my eyes rolled up in the back of my head and I passed out.

I COULD HEAR SOMEONE TALKING TO ME, BUT IT WAS MUFFLED. I could feel consciousness coming back slowly, but I still couldn't move.

"Sybil," Audrey whispered in a soft voice somewhere near me. "I know you can hear me. It's time to wake up. Wake up, sleepy troll," she said as she sobbed. "Please wake up."

I wanted to answer her, but I couldn't control my body.

"Geoffrey, Giles, Hugh, and I here waiting for you to wake up," she continued.

Some feeling started returning to my body, but it was mostly pain.

"You need to wake up," she said, sounding angry. "I can't sit here and watch you die! You have to wake up and talk to me!" she screamed.

My eyes finally opened and I groaned in pain. "Sybil!" everyone yelled at once.

I slowly lifted my hand and looked at the large bruise on my palm where I had been holding the ball. "How?" I croaked and then groaned in pain from talking on my raw throat.

"Geoffrey found you and cut the vines off, but you had already soaked up a lot of poison. It took the healers a long time to get it out," Audrey told me, tears in her eyes.

Gerard/Geoffrey handed me a cup of water and helped me sit up. I drank from the cup slowly, avoiding his eyes.

"We postponed your mother's funeral until you were better," Hugh said.

"Thank you," I whispered and then instantly regretted speaking at all.

"You shouldn't talk for a while," Giles said. "Just rest." He patted my knee and then left the room.

Audrey hugged me and then she and Hugh headed out together, leaving me alone with Gerard/Geoffrey. He sat silently beside me for a moment and then said, "I'm sorry I didn't tell you everything."

I made a writing motion and he grabbed a piece of paper and pen and handed them to me. I wrote: *I'm sorry I thought you were a traitor. Charles had been putting those thoughts into my head and so...I'm sorry*

He read the note and half crumpled it as he clenched his fist. He straightened the paper out and said, "It's alright. I would have been suspicious too."

I took the paper back and wrote: *Do you hate me now?*

He read it and laughed softly. "Of course not." He tilted my chin up, forcing me to meet his eyes. "Do you hate me?"

I shook my head and before he could try to kiss me I wrote: *What do I call you?*

He smiled. "Geoffrey is my true name."

I took the paper back and wrote: *Nice to meet you Prince Geoffrey.*

He shook his head. "I'm still the same person. I just have a different name."

Are you going back to your Troupe to rule it? I wrote and forced myself to keep a straight face as I gave it to him.

He read it and looked up at me. His eyes searched over my face a moment and then he asked, "Is that what you want me to do? Do you want me to leave?"

What did I want him to do? I felt betrayed by him, yet I knew Charles was the real traitor. Just because it had been his father that killed Octavius and my mother didn't mean I should hold it against Geoffrey.

Do you want to stay? I wrote instead of answering.

"My feelings haven't changed. If anything, they've only intensified," he answered. "The only question left is, what do *you* want to do?"

I set the pen and paper down and met his eyes. "Want," I croaked and then had to take a drink of water to soothe my throat.

"Shh, don't talk, Sybil," he said and handed me back the paper and pen. I shook my head and felt tears falling down my face. I wanted to talk. I wanted to be able to actually *tell* him. "Write it down."

I reluctantly took the pen and wrote: *I want to be with you, but you're a prince. There are customs and laws about a prince and princess courting from different troupes.*

"You're queen now," he said. "Not princess. And I'm not from that troupe. I may have been born there, but I was raised here for the majority of my life. I don't hold any feelings for that court. Do you still want me to be your guard?"

I shook my head and he jerked back in pain. I quickly wrote down: *You can't be my Guard since you're of a royal bloodline.*

He read the note and then looked up at me, eyes wide and pained. "You're serious?"

I nodded my head and then scribbled quickly: *You would have to become King if you wanted to be with me.*

He stared at the note and frowned. "Oh."

I had been a fool to think he'd want that. I set the pen and paper down and stood up, promptly falling to my knees. Geoffrey reached out to me, but I held my hand out stopping him. I pushed up and walked to the window, looking out over the growers and their fields. I sniffed as tears slid down my face and I felt my heart breaking again. How much could one heart handle?

"Why are you crying?" he asked as he turned me around.

I turned my face away from his and wiped at my eyes. He held out a small box to me. "Your birthday present," he whispered. "I didn't get to give it to you on your birthday."

I took it from him and slowly opened it. Inside was a beautiful ring with a silver gem I'd never seen before. I looked up at him only to find him sliding down to one knee. "Sybil of the Northern Troupe, will you become my queen?" he asked.

I looked from the ring to him and then did the only thing I could. I dropped down and kissed him. He kissed me back and I could feel his smile against my lips. He pulled back just long enough to slip the ring on my finger and then we were kissing again.

"Is that a yes?" he asked as we broke apart again.

I nodded my head fast and then hugged him, enjoying being wrapped inside his wings like a cocoon of safety.

"Sybil!" Hugh yelled as he entered the room. "Oh, uh, sorry," he muttered when he finally saw us.

Geoffrey helped me stand and I walked to Hugh. I raised my arms in the air to ask what.

"We caught Charles."

I pushed him to the side and rushed out the door.

"Sybil, wait!" Geoffrey called as he ran up to me. I reached back for my sword and cursed in my head when I realized it wasn't there. I motioned for his sword and he shook his head. "No."

I pointed at myself then at him then at me and then at his sword trying to convey I order you to give me your sword.

"No. I am not giving you my sword," he repeated as he held open the door for me and Hugh. I turned to Hugh, but Geoffrey pulled me away. "No. Just trust me, okay?"

I wasn't sure why he wouldn't give me the sword, but I nodded my head, agreeing to trust him. We stepped into the courtyard and I was shocked to see it back to normal. I hadn't thought there would still be bodies, but I also hadn't expected it to be so clean and look as though nothing had even happened. Adam and another of the warriors named Phil, whom was a total egotistical jerk, were holding Charles between them.

Charles looked up and stared at me, blinking. "You're alive?"

"Release him," Geoffrey said.

Adam and Phil looked at me and I nodded my head. They reluctantly released Charles and stepped back. Charles brushed himself off and then charged at Geoffrey. Geoffrey easily side-stepped his rushed punch and then thrust his sword into Charles' stomach. Part of me was revolted at the ease of his killing while the other part of me wished I had been the one to kill him.

"She's mine and has always been mine," Geoffrey told Charles who was staring at the sword in his stomach. "I thought you should know we're getting married."

Charles looked at the ring on my finger and then yelled, "No!" He fell to the ground and before he could speak again Geoffrey thrust his sword into Charles' heart. I had to look away as I tried not to remember doing the same thing to Octavius.

"Toss him over the cliff," Geoffrey told Adam. "He doesn't deserve to be buried in the woods with our other dead."

I felt so betrayed and so miserable that all I wanted to do was crawl into bed and sleep. "Sybil?" Geoffrey whispered. I couldn't be the lazy princess anymore though. My days of childish play were over. Now I was Queen of the Northern Troupe of Fairies.

I turned to Geoffrey and met his eyes. My throat still hurt so I couldn't talk, but as I stared into his eyes, he smiled and I knew he understood. He pulled me gently against his chest and kissed the top of my head. "We will rule together and together we will make this Troupe the strongest and most loving Troupe ever." He paused a moment and then whispered, "I love you, Sybil."

I looked up at him and smiled as I whispered, "I know. I love you too."

AFTERWORD

THANK YOU FOR READING MY BOOK. IF YOU ENJOYED IT, WON'T YOU PLEASE CONSIDER LEAVING A REVIEW?

MORE FROM CATHERINE BANKS

Calvin's Alien Adventure

Pirate Princess Trilogy
Pirate Princess
Princess Triumvirate
Pirate Queen*

Little Death Bringer Duology
Mercenary
Protector
Little Death Bringer, The Official Coloring Book*

Her Royal Harem Series
Royally Entangled
Royally Exposed
Royally Elected
Royally Enraged
Her Royal Harem, The Complete Series
The Demon's Fair
Her Royal Harem, The Coloring Book*

Zodiac Shifters Paranormal Romance Series
Centaur's Prize
Tiger Tears
Lion About

Demonic Contract
Anja's Secret
Daughter of Lions
Dragon's Blood
The Last Werewolf
Last Ama Princess
Transforming Rose
Lady Serra and the Draconian
Alys of Asgard
Phoenix Possessed
Sybil Deceived
The Pawn
Stone Heart

The Lioness's Harem Trilogy
Lonely Lioness

Anderelle: Minloa Trilogy
Queen of the Stars
Goddess of the Universe*

*COMING SOON

CONNECT WITH CATHERINE BANKS

I really appreciate you reading my book! Here are some ways to connect with me:

www.catherinebanks.com

Follow me on BookBub: https://www.bookbub.com/authors/catherine-banks

Join my newsletter for deals and snippets: http://catbanks.co/newsletter

Like my author Facebook page: http://www.Facebook.com/CatherineBanksAuthor

Follow me on Twitter: http://www.Twitter.com/catherineebanks

Follow me on Goodreads: http://www.Goodreads.com/catherine_banks

Purchase items handmade by Catherine: http://Etsy.com/shop/TurboKittenInd